A Gift For: _____

From: _____

Copyright © 2016 Hallmark Licensing, LLC

Published by Hallmark Gift Books,
a division of Hallmark Cards, Inc.,
Kansas City, MO 64141
Visit us on the Web at Hallmark.com.

Editorial Director: Delia Berrigan
Editor: Kim Schworm Acosta
Art Director: Chris Opheim
Designer: Laura Elsenraat
Production Designer: Dan Horton

ISBN: 978-1-63059-941-6
XKT1695

Made in China
0716

Magical Sleigh? SNOW WAY!

Written by Diana Manning   Illustrated by Mike Esberg

Hallmark

Christmas is coming! And here in Chill Valley,
they don't waste a minute—they don't dillydally.
There's the hanging of lights and the holiday shopping,
errands to run and the Christmas-tree chopping!

Sometimes it seems there's so much to be done,
there's hardly time left for the best part . . . the FUN!
But magical things are about to occur,
all thanks to a snowkid named Freezy McBrrr.

Now, Freezy spends time in the family shop—
a quirky garage where ideas never stop.
They take worn-out sleighs and they fix 'em like new
for people to come in and buy when they're through.

Freezy loves helping . . . there's so much to do.

His kid sister Frozemary likes to help, too.

Their dad lets them add their own touch to each sleigh—
though Freezy can sometimes get carried away!

One day an old spray can of paint caught his eye—
"Go ahead," said his dad. "Why not give it a try?"
It said "Christmas Spirit" in letters of red,
so he gave it a go, just like his dad said.

When Freezy was finished, that sleigh started rocking—
it rattled and shook in a way that was shocking!
As Freezy jumped into the seat in a hurry,
away went the sleigh in a flash and a flurry!

Nobody knew what was making it go, but boy,
was it fun as it swooshed through the snow . . .
it seemed to go anywhere Freezy desired—
at just the right pace, with no reindeer required!

Word got around about Freezy's new sleigh,
and everyone wanted a ride right away!
The family pitched in as the riders lined up—
Mom served them cocoa in Christmas-y cups.

Grandma and Grandpa stepped in for a ride . . .
they wanted to go for a leisurely glide.

But not Uncle Fridge and Aunt Arctica . . . no!

They wanted that sleigh to just go-go-go-GO!

The snowpeople waited their turn all day long—
that sleigh held some magic that must have been strong.
In line, they all chatted with friends old and new,
while snowkids shared treats and built snowcastles, too!

That night after everyone else had gone home,
Freezy and Dad took a ride of their own,
stopping to look at the beautiful lights—
their favorite tradition on holiday nights.

"Christmas is awesome! And so is this sleigh!"
said Freezy to Dad as they slid on their way.
"But what made it magically go by itself?"
"It was you," Dad replied, "and your choice from the shelf!"

Clink!

"You know, Christmas Spirit is powerful stuff.

Sometimes just a dab or a spritz is enough.

You helped the whole town take the time for some fun—

you gave them a gift, and I'm proud of you, Son!"

So Freezy helped all of Chill Valley to see

how special the time spent with others can be.

They're never too busy for fun anymore,

'cause they know in their hearts, that's what Christmas is for!

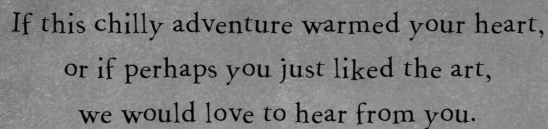

If this chilly adventure warmed your heart,
or if perhaps you just liked the art,
we would love to hear from you.

Please send your comments to:
Hallmark Book Feedback
P.O. Box 419034
Mail Drop 100
Kansas City, MO 64141

Or e-mail us at:
booknotes@hallmark.com

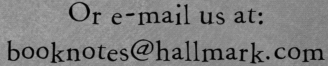